RETREAT FROM MURDER

TRASH TO TREASURE COZY MYSTERIES, BOOK 4

DONNA CLANCY

SUMMER PRESCOTT BOOKS PUBLISHING

To all who believe and search for those on the other side.

CHAPTER ONE

"I look forward to this weekend every year," Sage said.

"I do, too," Gabby replied, throwing a lightweight jacket into her suitcase. "My mom and I don't get to spend a lot of time together, which makes this weekend even more special to me."

"My mom gets so excited every time she's able to go ghost hunting, even though we've been to the lighthouse eight years in a row, and she's never seen a thing," Sage said. "Just once, I wish she would see the ghost of Captain Wells while we're there."

"Maybe that's what you hope for, but I, for one, don't want to run into anything or anyone who's dead and still moving around. I just want a quiet weekend with my mom, walking the beach and drinking wine."

"Who knows, if you drink enough wine you may see some ghosts," Sage said, laughing.

"Very funny. Are you all packed?"

"I am. I have all my ghostbusting regalia and am ready to go," she answered, teasing her friend. "Seriously, I packed last night because I had some last-minute deliveries to make this morning before we left."

"I know, rub it in why don't you?" Gabby zipped up her suitcase and set it on the floor. "I really wanted the dining room ensemble you just finished. The black chairs with the silver and turquoise upholstered seats were to die for. And the matching black hutch, total class. Even Rory said he would have loved to have the set which says a lot, because normally he couldn't care less about furniture."

"I'm sorry. Mrs. Snow brought me the material and asked if I could create her a dining room around it. I do have some of the material left over if you want me to make you something using it. Maybe a new bench for your vanity?" Sage suggested, glancing at the threadbare one sitting in front of them.

"That would be awesome! You do realize if you paint the bench black, you'll have to paint the vanity, too?"

"I know, another wedding gift." Sage rolled her eyes.

"You're the best," Gabby said, hugging her best friend. "If you paint the vanity black, the bed will have to be painted to match it, too."

"Let's go before you find something else for me to do," Sage said, picking up the suitcase and walking out of the room before Gabby could reply.

"I'm going to call the salon one more time before we leave. This is the first time I've left for three days and gone any distance away. I believe Cheryl and Cindy can handle things, but I want to see if they have any last-minute questions," Gabby said, already dialing.

"While you make your call, I'm going to get the stuff out of the van and lock it up," Sage said, standing up from where she sat on the front porch. "I'm glad we're going in your mom's SUV. It's such a nice ride after spending all my driving time in an old cargo van that has no suspension left and rattles terribly."

"And hers has air-conditioning," Gabby added.

"Yes! The air-conditioning in my van consists of rolling down the windows and going a little faster to whip up the breeze." Sage laughed. "But it serves its purpose when it comes to moving furniture."

"You could get a used car to putz around in for everyday use and drive your van for work."

"I could, but I don't want to hurt Benny's feelings by replacing him and letting him sit in the driveway most of the time," Sage said.

"Really?" Gabby held a finger in the air. "Hello? Cindy…"

Sage grabbed her suitcase and set it next to Gabby's on the porch. Her friend was still on the phone as her mom drove into the circular driveway. Lou exited her car and popped the hatch while Sage grabbed the two suitcases and added them to the one already in the back.

LouAnn, who preferred to be called Lou, was a young looking sixty-year-old. Gabby was the younger version of her mom. Both were slender in build, athletic, had brown hair and could talk your ear off. Dressed in cut-offs, a tank top, and flip-flops, she could have passed for Gabby's sister instead of her mother.

"Are we ready to go?" Lou asked.

"We were until your daughter made a phone call to the salon."

"Don't you worry. Once I get her in the car, she won't think about the salon all weekend," Lou promised. "Gabby! Let's go!"

"I'll be right there."

"I stopped at the liquor store and got some new wines for us to try over the weekend," Lou said when she closed the hatch.

"Great minds think alike," Sage said, holding up her beach bag. "I did, too."

"Okay, everything is set at the salon. This weekend is going to be so awesome, especially after all the chaos surrounding Madam Hand and her salon. I need some time away." Gabby climbed in the backseat of her mom's car.

"Off we go! Next stop is *This and That* to pick up Sarah," Lou said, putting the car in gear.

A short time later, they pulled up in front of the thrift shop. Sarah and her employee and friend, Flora, were sitting on the front patio having coffee. Sage jumped out to grab her mom's suitcase and thanked Flora for watching the shop so her mom could go away for the weekend and not worry about anything. Flora assured them that she loved the shop as much as Sarah did and would take care of the place like it was her own. When everyone was settled in, and Sarah was in the front seat with Lou, the four women drove off for their long weekend adventure.

Moosehead Light was located on the easternmost-furthest point of Moosehead. The lighthouse itself had been built in 1859 and the keeper's quarters, where the women would be sleeping, was added on sometime later, but the records of the property don't say exactly when it was built. It is assumed it was sometime around 1863. At that time, the first keeper was assigned to man the lighthouse and started to keep daily records which were now archived with the historical society.

Captain Jedidiah Wells was the first paid keeper of Moosehead Light. He was a whaling captain, but his ship went down in bad weather. He and a handful of his men survived when they were fished out of the ocean by another passing whaler. Instead of pushing his luck and captaining another ship at his age, he retired. Because of his background, he was hired as the lighthouse keeper and paid quite handsomely for it.

It is rumored another local wanted the job Captain Wells received. Stephen Holmes was quite vocal at the time, insisting he had lived in Moosehead his whole life unlike the captain who moved there after he retired. He felt the job should have been his as he had been maintaining the structure for over ten years and not been paid for doing it.

The story passed down over time was that Holmes figured if the old man died, he would get the job. He entered the residence when Wells went to town for his monthly supplies and poisoned the whiskey he drank every evening as his nightcap. The captain was found dead in his cottage two days later, when someone from town checked on him because the light had gone out in the lighthouse.

Holmes was never caught as it was assumed at the time that the captain died of old age. The whiskey bottle containing the poison mysteriously disappeared before the body was found. It is said Captain Wells haunts the keeper's cottage because his killer was never held responsible for his murder even though the true story came out fifty years later.

Holmes did get the job and it is said Wells' ghost drove him crazy while he lived there. Entries in the daily journals admitted what Holmes did to get the job and how the ghost would never let him be until he wrote he would take his own life by jumping from the lighthouse. The final entry tells of how Holmes had one last night of peace. His body was found at the base of the lighthouse the next day. The captain finally got his revenge.

"I love the story of the lighthouse," Sage said, looking over the folder they had been sent from the owners with their reservation numbers and dining seating times. "Do you think you'll see Captain Wells this year, Mom?"

"You never know. He's been seen both in the keeper's quarters and the lighthouse. I guess you have to be in the right place at the right time to witness his ghost."

"You do all the ghost hunting you want. I'll be on the beach with my big glass of wine catching some rays," Gabby stated.

"I'm curious about the new owners that bought the place over the winter. They didn't change much according to the fliers, not even the prices," Sarah said. "You'd think with a new mortgage the prices would have increased."

"I'm going to miss the Dunbars. Patricia always picked out the best wines for us to sample during the wine tastings. She used to go to France and purchase them there on her vacation over the winter," Lou added.

"Even if the new owners aren't into wine like Patricia was, we brought enough of our own," Sage said, patting the beach bag at her feet. "They did change one thing. Instead of just the four of us in our room we do have another mother and daughter staying with us."

"I didn't even notice that when I read through the

packet. I hope they're not killjoys," Sarah said. "I kind of liked having the room to ourselves."

"I'm sure it will be fine," Gabby said. "Mom and I will be out on the beach most of the time anyway."

"I'll be exploring and only in the room to change and sleep," Sarah replied. "Besides, there is a nice common room for us to sit in at night if we want to talk."

"I don't have any set plans," Sage said, leaning her head back on the seat and closing her eyes. "Except maybe for taking a walk into town and getting Cliff some of the saltwater taffy he asked me to pick up for him."

"Was that the agreed upon pay-off for him watching the cats while we're gone?" Gabby asked.

"It was. A small price to pay for a long weekend of no worries," Sage replied.

"I might take that walk with you if you are going to the Moosehead Fudge Factory to get the taffy. I think I feel a craving coming on too for a couple of pounds of fudge to bring home," Gabby said. "Penuche, no nuts for me and chocolate with nuts for Rory."

"Pounds?" Lou asked.

"Yes, pounds. You can freeze it you know," her

daughter replied. "I still have some leftover from Christmas."

"Anyone object if I turn on the radio?" Sarah asked.

After a chorus of no's, music filled the car for the remainder of the ride to Moosehead. Half an hour later, their car turned onto Horseshoe Crab Lane. There were several cars ahead of them parked at the front door to unload their suitcases and check in.

"We can pull our own suitcases," Sage said. "Why don't we just park and walk to the office to check in?"

"Sounds good to me," Lou answered, pulling the car out of line and driving to the main parking lot.

"What a gorgeous day!" Sarah said, yanking her suitcase up over the edge of the curb. "Unlike last year when it rained two of the three days we were here."

"We had fun anyway. We played boardgames, drank wine and did some reading," Gabby replied. "Patricia made sure we had lots of indoor activities to participate in when we couldn't go to the beach."

"I have to admit, bingo was fun. I won a back scrubber that I still use in my shower every morning," Sage said.

"And I won a set of wine glasses Patricia brought back from Italy," Lou added.

"I didn't win a thing," Sarah complained.

"If I recall, after the first game you left and went ghost hunting," Lou replied. "It's kind of hard to win anything if you don't play."

The others laughed.

"She's got you there, Mom."

"Next!" the lady behind the front desk yelled.

"I'll check us in," Lou said.

"We're only five feet away. Did she have to yell like that?" Gabby whispered to Sage. "I wonder where Nellie is and how come she's not on the desk anymore."

Lou's voice got louder at the desk. The clerk looked none too pleased as the conversation progressed.

"Let's go see what's going on," Sage suggested.

The three women approached the desk and gathered around Lou. The clerk's face became even more contorted when she saw she would have to deal with more than one woman.

"Is there a problem?" Sarah asked.

"According to this woman we have no reservation," Lou replied. "I tried to show her the processed charge on my charge card, and she won't even look at it. All she keeps saying is we are not in the computer, and we have to leave."

"I'd like to talk to the owner, please," Sage requested loudly.

The desk clerk insisted she would not bother the owner for a matter as trivial as this and again requested the women leave.

"You WILL call the owner now," Sage insisted.

"Very well, but she's not going to be happy that she was bothered," the clerk said, shrugging her shoulders and picking up the phone.

The clerk turned her back to the group while she spoke on the phone.

"Maybe you'd better handle this instead of me," Lou said to Sage. "You are much better at dealing with disagreeable people than I am."

Sage stepped forward as the clerk hung up the phone.

"The owner will be right down. Please step aside so I can check-in the people who do have reservations," the clerk stated nastily.

"Excuse me?" Sage asked, leaning on the counter and not moving.

"Is there a problem here?" a well-dressed woman asked coming up behind Sage.

"There are several problems. First, you need to train your desk clerk not to be so nasty when dealing with your customers. If I owned this place and she spoke to my visitors like she spoke to us, she'd have been fired on the spot," Sage said, crossing her arms, glaring at the clerk.

"We'll speak later," she said to the clerk. "Now, Cassidy tells me you are here for a long weekend but have no reservations?"

"We made and paid for reservations last year when we left. This is our eighth year here and we always book the last weekend in June," Sage replied.

"I see the problem. You booked this place last year. We bought the business this past January and all the computer records were cleared with the sale. May I please see your receipt?"

She scanned the printed receipt that contained the paid charge amount.

"You do realize that by law, I don't have to honor this because your money should have been refunded by the previous owner before the sale went through. Let me see," she said, looking at the computer. "This may be a problem. You paid for a private room with two queen-sized beds, but this is the weekend before the Fourth and we are pretty much booked solid. The only thing I have open is a room with three bunkbeds and one other couple is already in there. If that is satisfactory you can stay, if not, I'm sorry but I will not refund your money."

"By couple do you mean a man and a woman?" Sage asked.

"No, I mean two women. Sisters, I believe. And the room is located in the base of the lighthouse. I'm afraid that's all I have to offer you."

"What I don't understand is you sent us a dinner schedule for our seating time not a month ago. How come we were in the computer then but not now?" Sage asked.

"A glitch, I guess. Do you want the room or not?"

"Or overbooking," Sage said under her breath, turning to her group. "Do you want to stay in the lighthouse, in bunkbeds?"

"It might be fun to stay in the lighthouse," Gabby said. "Mom?"

"As long as I get a bottom bunk I don't have a problem with it," Lou replied.

"I might have a better chance of seeing the captain if we stay in the lighthouse," Sarah said. "I'm in. We're already here so why not?"

"Perfect. Sign this registration card for your group and I'll get your keys," the owner said, shoving a card toward Sage.

"Do you have an activities chart for in-house events while we're here?" Sage asked, filling in the card. "Patricia used to have the best wine tastings when we stayed here."

"We offer no activities. There are more than enough things to do around town. We offer you a place to sleep and two meals a day, breakfast and dinner."

"Nothing like Patricia, is she?" Gabby whispered to her mother.

"I have a feeling we'll be finding a new place to vacation after this year," Lou whispered back.

"Here's the two keys. Enjoy your stay," the owner said, turning on one foot and walking away.

"Next!" the desk clerk yelled.

"I suppose nothing good lasts forever," Sage said, rejoining her group. "She didn't even introduce herself. Well, let's make the best of the weekend we can, and we'll probably have to find a new place next year."

"I was just saying the same thing to Gabby," Lou said.

Luckily, the women knew their way around after having spent so many vacations there and were at the door of the lighthouse quickly. Sarah located the door to the lower level. Once inside, a door straight ahead of them led to the bunk room. There were two middle-aged women already in the room who turned to see who else was entering.

The room was almost bare. Three sets of bunkbeds that looked like they had been there for a hundred years, four folding chairs and a card table and a tiny refrigerator were all that was in the room. A wooden floor had been haphazardly installed to cover the dirt floor underneath. The new owners tried to dress up the room with brightly colored comforters on the beds, but it just made the rest of the room look more dismal.

A full-sized bathroom complete with a walk-in shower, toilet and sink was off to the right. It wasn't a good fit for six women being in the same room and all having to use the same bathroom to get ready or change when needed.

"Looks like someone else made reservations last year and got bounced out to the lighthouse," one of them said. "Hi, I'm Angie and this is my sister Beverly."

"I remember you. We were all at the wine tasting together," Gabby said.

"Yes, we were. Pat made things so fun around here, unlike now," Beverly replied.

"We so agree," Lou said, placing her suitcase at the foot of one of the bunk beds. "Gabby, you win the top bunk. You're younger than I am and can crawl up there easier."

"I'll take the top, Mom, even though I know you can easily get up and down from there," Gabby said, laughing.

"I'll take the top bunk, too," Sage said.

"I can't believe we have to deal with bunk beds and stay in a cellar," Angie said, frowning. "I tried to get our money back to go somewhere else and she refused."

"If you don't mind me asking, just exactly who are the new owners?" Lou asked.

"Don and Meredith Randall. I'm not sure where they moved here from, but they should have stayed where they were," Angie grumbled.

"They don't seem too well suited for the hospitality world," Sarah agreed. "Nor their desk clerk."

"Let's not let them ruin our weekend," Gabby said. "Anyone want a glass of wine?"

"Don't let the Randalls know you have wine in the room. It's against their rules. They confiscated ours and said we could have it back when we left on Sunday."

"They took your wine? It's a good thing they didn't see ours in the beach bags," Gabby said.

"I even followed her to try to get it back and she

all but physically shoved me out of her office. It appears she doesn't get along with too many people as she was arguing with some man who was sitting at her desk. I'm afraid if you want to drink here you have to buy it from them at the bar," Beverly stated.

"I guess it will be our little secret then," Gabby said, breaking open a package of plastic tumblers. "At least we have a small refrigerator for the wine."

She poured six glasses of wine and passed them out.

"To a great weekend despite the new owners," Sage said, holding her glass up in a toast.

"Hear, hear," the rest joined in.

"I guess we'll be living out of our suitcases," Lou said, looking around for bureaus.

"It's only for a few days, Mom. I think we'll manage," her daughter replied. "I'm going to head out to the beach. Anyone coming with me?"

"This is my only vacation. I'm going to start it out by taking a nice nap," Sarah said.

"That sounds good to me," Beverly said. "I think I'll join you."

"I'm up for a walk on the beach. I need some shells for a project I'm working on at home," Sage stated.

"I'll join you, if you don't mind," Angie asked. "I love to gather shells."

"You're more than welcome to come with us," Lou replied.

The four women left for their walk leaving Sarah and Beverly to nap.

"I love this beach," Gabby said, looking up at the sun. "The water is so clean, and the sand is so pristine. I wonder if they still have the beach chairs that you can use while you stay here."

"I don't see them set up anywhere out here on the beach the way they used to be. Maybe you have to ask for them now," Sage said.

"I'll sit on a towel before I ask that old crank behind the desk to use a chair," Gabby stated, frowning.

"No more grumbling. Let's take that walk and get some shells for Sage," Lou said, dropping her sandals into her beach bag. "The sand is so warm. My toes love it!"

The four women walked for the next couple of hours. The beach stretched a good two miles behind other bed and breakfasts and hotels. There were many families enjoying their vacations in and out of the water. Sage had a full bag of shells when they finally returned to the lighthouse.

Sarah was up, reading and enjoying more wine. Beverly was still napping. Sarah shushed the women as they entered the room.

"It's almost time for supper," Lou whispered.

"You women go ahead. I'll wait for Beverly to wake up and then we'll join you," Angie told them pulling a book out of her suitcase. "Remember, don't tell anyone you have wine in the room."

"We'll see you in the dining room," Sage said.

The women asked for a table that seated six for when Angie and Beverly joined them. They perused the wine menu and ordered a bottle of wine that would go with anything that was ordered. The waitress came back with the wine and pulled out a pad to take their orders.

Sage and her mother ordered swordfish cooked in lemon and garlic butter. Their sides were baked sweet potatoes cooked with maple syrup and brown sugar along with a helping of summer squash. Gabby ordered broiled scallops cooked in white wine with fries and coleslaw.

Lou decided to really splurge and ordered the fisherman's platter which had every kind of seafood on it that you could imagine. Fried clams, scallops, flounder, and shrimp along with calamari and a lobster tail made up the mainstay of the platter. It came with onion rings and a side of coleslaw.

"You will never finish all that," Gabby said, laughing, when the waitress set the platter in front of her mother. "That's enough for four people to eat."

"It is. And it's a good thing there is a small fridge and a microwave in the room so I can enjoy every bit of it over the weekend while we're here," Lou said. "May I please get some extra drawn butter and cock-tail sauce when you get a chance?"

"This food is to die for," Gabby stated, plopping a scallop in her mouth.

Half-way through their meal, a frantic scream rang out for help.

CHAPTER TWO

"Someone help me!" Angie screamed, running into the dining room. "Beverly's not breathing! I think she's dead!"

Sage and Gabby were the first ones to reach Angie.

"Please help me. Something's not right. My sister…"

"I'm a doctor," another diner said, approaching the women. "Take me to where your sister is."

The four women followed behind the doctor who entered the room with Angie while they stayed at the door. A minute later they were joined by the owners, Don and Meredith Randall.

"What's going on?" Meredith demanded to know.

"Something is wrong with Beverly," Lou whispered.

"I'm so sorry," the man said, turning to face Angie. "I'm afraid she is gone."

"No, it can't be. She was in perfect health. What happened to her?' Angie asked, tears flowing down her cheeks. "I don't believe this."

Angie ran from the room. Lou followed her figuring the poor woman was in shock and wanted to know if she was okay.

"My first assessment says it was natural causes, but without an autopsy we won't know," the doctor replied. "Don, please call the police and tell them to send the coroner's wagon."

Don left to make the phone call. Gabby and Sarah sat at the card table while they waited for the police to arrive. Meredith hurried away to calm the rest of the patrons who were in the dining room when Angie burst in, screaming for help. Sage walked around the room as if searching for something.

"What are you doing?" Sarah asked her daughter.

"Don't you smell that?"

"Smell what?"

"It smells like bitter almonds. It's very faint but I can smell it now and I didn't when we were in the room before," Sage answered.

She spotted a small jewelry box sitting on the table and walked to it. She picked it up and smelled it keeping it quite a distance from her face.

"Where did this box come from?" Sage asked, dropping it on the table. "Don't anyone touch it."

"We were finishing our wine before our nap and a knock sounded on the door. Beverly went to answer it and found the box on the mat outside the door."

"By itself? No one was out there delivering it?" Sage asked.

"No, no one was there. She picked up the box and the note it was sitting on. It asked Beverly to forgive the way she was treated when she went to the office and to accept the earrings as a gift. It was signed Meredith."

"Where are the earrings?"

"Beverly put them on immediately. They were the cutest little lighthouses. Then we laid down to take our naps."

The doctor took out a handkerchief and picked up the box. He took one smell and wrapped the box in his handkerchief so no one else would touch it.

"Go wash your hands right now!" he said to Sage. "I think your friend has been poisoned."

"Poisoned? By whom and why?" Gabby gasped.

"I don't know, but Sage is right. I smell the odor

of bitter almonds on the inside of the jewelry box and that particular smell can be a sign of cyanide."

"Clear the room, please," a police officer requested from the door. "But don't go far as we need to ask some of you questions."

The doctor walked over to the officer, taking the wrapped box with him, and requested to speak to him outside. They returned several minutes later, the officer frowning. The box was now in an evidence bag.

"Who was the one in the room with the deceased when the gift was delivered?"

"I was," Sarah answered. "She was fine when we laid down for our naps."

"Where is the note that was delivered with the earrings?"

"Right here," Sage said, holding up the piece of paper. "I don't think it will be of any use to you. If someone is going to poison a person, they wouldn't sign their real name to a note."

"Who is Meredith?" the officer asked.

"Don and Meredith are friends of mine. They bought this place over the winter. Meredith can be an unfriendly, gruff person, but I have known them a long time and I don't think she would ever poison anyone," the doctor added.

"We don't even know if the victim was poisoned yet. We won't know until the coroner does an autopsy, and the earrings are tested. This is a potential crime scene, and no one can stay here. Other arrangements need to be made for accommodations for the rest of you," the officer said. "And please don't discuss the earrings with anyone outside of this room."

"Why are the police here?" Meredith asked, returning from the dining room with her husband in tow. "This is not good for business."

"And you would be?" the officer asked.

"Meredith Randall."

"Meredith, huh? Are you the Meredith in question who sent the gift to the deceased?"

"What are you talking about? I never sent a gift to anyone," she stammered.

"You didn't send lighthouse earrings to Beverly Simpson as an apology for mistreating her when she came to your office?"

"I did not! She was in my office, but she talked to Don more than she did me. I showed her the way out when I caught them hugging again," Meredith stated. "And on her way out she also insisted I give her back the confiscated wine from earlier. There is no drinking in the rooms. Rules are rules."

"I explained to my wife the hugs were simply

between old friends seeing each other again," Don replied. "And the drinking rule is a stupid one. People are on vacation and want to relax."

"They can relax as long as they pay for their drinks at our bar," Meredith threw back at her husband. "We are in business to make money."

"This place won't be in business long," Sage mumbled under her breath, getting the evil eye from Meredith.

"These people need to be assigned to another room until the room can be processed," the officer said.

"We don't have any open rooms. This is the weekend before the Fourth and we are booked solid. They will have to find somewhere else to go," Meredith said, glaring at Sage.

"Not true. The Baileys just cancelled so their room is open. We can put an additional cot in the room. If that is okay with you ladies," Don offered much to the chagrin of his wife.

"I'm afraid I won't be staying at this place, now or ever again. I have arrangements to make on my sister's behalf and must tell our family. I will be staying down the street at the Sea and Sand Hotel on Main Street until they release my sister's body, and I can take her home," Angie said, returning with Lou and standing at the door.

"I am so sorry for your loss. Would you please give your cell information to one of my officers outside before you leave?" the officer requested. "We'll need you to come to the station for questioning."

"The coroner is here," one of the officers said, leaning in the open door. "Should I send him in?"

"Please do. I will let the owners know when you can return to the room to clear out your things."

"We'll be in the bar. Our supper has probably been cleared away for the second shift of diners," Lou said. "Angie, I am so sorry about your sister. Please take care of yourself and be well."

Each person gave their condolences on the way out except for Meredith. She was too busy arguing with her husband about offering the empty room that they could have rented out for the weekend.

"Meredith, please stay behind as we have more questions for you. And your husband as well," the officer requested.

"I have things that need attending to," she replied.

"Those things can wait, or we can take this down to the station and continue our questioning there. Which will it be?"

"Very well," she stated, not happy in the least.

The four friends sat in the corner of the bar with their wine. No one spoke for several minutes until Gabby broke the silence.

"Could Meredith have been that jealous over a hug that she would kill poor Beverly?"

"It doesn't seem likely. Did you see her face? She looked as surprised as all of us did when she entered the room and saw the police there," Sage replied. "I think someone is trying to frame Meredith. As much as I don't like the woman or her ways, I don't think it was her."

"Then again, we don't even know if Beverly has been poisoned," Lou said. "Sarah, tell us exactly what happened after we left the room."

"Please do. I would like to hear your version also," the same officer who had been in the room requested.

"After you left to go for your walk on the beach, Beverly and I poured ourselves a glass of wine and took out the books we were reading. Maybe ten minutes later there was a knock on the door. Beverly answered it and discovered the little package with a note underneath it left outside on the mat. She brought them inside and read the note out loud to me."

"The same note signed by Meredith?" Sage asked.

"Yes, that was the one."

"Did she say if she saw anyone lurking outside watching as she picked up the gift?" Sage asked.

"She didn't say. After she read me the note, she held up the little lighthouse earrings for me to see and put them in her ears. A minute later she said she was going to lay down and forego her reading," Sarah replied.

"Did she say she felt sick in any way?" the officer asked. "Cyanide can kill a person in anywhere from one to five minutes."

"No, she just went and laid down. I kept reading and assumed she was sleeping."

"And no one else came into the room that you know of?"

"I'm positive it was just Beverly and myself in the room. After a half hour of reading, I also laid down and took a short nap. When I woke up, I poured myself another glass of wine and started to read again. Beverly was still napping when the others returned so I hushed them as they came into the room. Am I a suspect because I was in the room alone with her?"

"We won't know anything until the earrings are

checked at the lab. You ladies will be staying for the entire weekend, yes?"

"You didn't answer my mother's question. Is she a suspect or not?" Sage asked.

"I'm sorry but yes, she is. It is her word only about the events that led up to the death, so I am afraid she is until we can prove otherwise," the officer said.

"We will be here until Monday morning," Sarah answered.

"I will be in touch," he said, rising to his feet to leave. "And please, I have to admonish you, do not mention the poisoned earrings to anyone else outside of this circle. We did not even tell the owners about the possibility of her being poisoned. There are certain facts the police like to keep quiet when investigating a murder."

"Well, this has turned out to be a vacation for the record books," Sarah said, sighing.

"The big question here is who has reason enough to frame Meredith and want her out of the way?" Sage said, pouring herself more wine.

"They always say look at the husband first," Lou pointed out. "You can tell he's henpecked and doesn't seem very happy with his current situation."

"True, but he does tend to stand up to her once in

a while. No, I don't think it's him," Sage said. "That would be too obvious. I am going to do a little checking around and see what the other employees think about their bosses."

"Are you going to talk to the grouch at the front desk?" Gabby asked.

"She's first on my list. I have found that disgruntled people are the first ones to talk about their bosses and current work situations. I have a feeling I can get a lot of information from her," Sage replied.

Don, followed by several waitresses approached the women. They had plates of various appetizers they set down on the table in front of the group.

"I figured since you didn't get to eat your supper you might be hungry. It's not a fisherman's platter but the food is tasty," Don said, smiling. "And please, accept my apologies for my wife's attitude. She is so wrapped up in making this place a success she tends to be a tad bit nasty sometimes."

"A tad bit?" Lou asked.

"Okay, a lot nasty. Deep down, she is a good person," Don replied, frowning. "In her defense, I must admit she does have some cause to be like she is. I had an affair many years ago and she has been on her guard ever since then. She says she forgives me, but sometimes I wonder if she really ever has."

"Excuse me for being straight forward with you, but was the affair with Beverly?" Sage asked.

"It was, but how did you know?" he asked.

"She caught you hugging the woman, not once but twice. And you still think she has no reason to be upset with Beverly? Maybe she thought the affair was picking up again," Sage replied.

"I truly thought about leaving Meredith for Beverly back when we had the affair, but I didn't. I stuck it out even though sometimes I wish I hadn't."

"Did you tell the police about the affair?" Sage asked.

"I didn't because I was afraid it would make Meredith look even more guilty. The police confided in me about the possibility of the earrings being poisoned. They told me I was not to discuss it with my wife or anyone else but to be careful. If she poisoned Beverly she could do the same thing to me out of revenge" he said, his shoulders drooping.

"If I were you, I'd drive right down to the station and tell them," Lou said, picking up a shrimp and dipping it into the cocktail sauce. "And thank you for the food, I was starving."

"You're so welcome. And thank you for all your advice. I'm going down to talk to the police as soon as I'm done here."

"For what it's worth, I don't think Meredith did it. I think someone is setting her up for the fall," Sage said. "Can you think of anyone who despises your wife enough to want her out of the way? Any other women in your life?"

"There has been no one else since Beverly. Are you saying you believe Meredith is innocent?"

"I am and I will find out who did it because they have my mom on the suspect list because she was the only one in the room with her when she died," Sage replied.

"Just tell me how I can help. In a way, I feel responsible for Beverly's death. If we hadn't had the affair, she might still be alive," he answered.

"Did you know that Angie and Beverly vacationed here every year before you bought the place?"

"No. When the sale went through all the customers who had reservations from the previous year were supposed to have their money returned so we would start with a clean slate. I had no idea Beverly, and her sister would be here, and I didn't know they had vacationed here before."

"Well, someone knew and put the sisters visit to good use," Gabby stated.

"Does anyone else know about your affair with Beverly?" Sage asked.

"No, it was many years ago and I don't know any of the current guests we have staying with us now."

"How about employees?"

"They are all new hires from the local area. The only one my wife knew and hired was Cassidy Black at the front desk. And she definitely wasn't my first pick to man the desk and greet the guests."

"I have to agree with you there," Gabby said. "She's pretty rude and she doesn't exactly give off a great first impression of the place."

"I know, but she's my wife's niece. She hasn't been able to hold down a job anywhere else, so we got stuck with her. My wife's sister demanded Meredith give her a job here."

"And there is no one else you can think of who might have it out for Meredith?" Sage asked again.

"No one."

"I do have a request. Once the police clear the crime scene I would like to continue staying in the lighthouse. I can move around more freely from there without prying eyes watching my every move. The rest of my group might want the nicer room you offered," Sage said.

"I'll stay in the lighthouse with you," her mother said. "I might have a better chance of seeing the ghost of Captain Wells if I stay out there."

"I for one don't want to see any old ghost," Gabby stated. "I'll stay in the offered room if that is okay."

"Lou, why don't you stay with Gabby?" Sarah suggested. "You can have some real mother daughter time without us around."

"Please, Mom. That's why I look forward to this long weekend in the first place," Gabby said.

"If Mr. Randall doesn't object to us taking up two spaces at the same time, I will gladly stay in the room with the queen-sized bed instead of a hard bunk," Lou replied.

"If Sage is willing to help prove my wife's innocence you can have any room available," Don said. "And please, call me Don."

"It's settled then. We may have to all stay in the new room tonight until the police clear the crime scene, but tomorrow night my mom and I will be sleeping in the lighthouse."

"And hopefully, seeing a ghost," Sarah added.

"Enjoy your food. I'm heading out to the police station right now. I will see you ladies in the morning. Have a better rest of the night."

They watched the owner walk away. Another bottle of wine was delivered to the group, no charge, from Don. The rest of the evening was spent eating, drinking, and laughing. They raised their glasses in a toast to Beverly even though they had only spent a few weekends together over the years.

The food was gone, and the wine bottles were empty. They went to the desk to find the location of their new room. Cassidy was not at the desk. A young gentleman, very mild mannered and polite greeted them as they approached. He gave them the keys to their new room along with the message the police had gone through all their belongings and had released them from custody. Mr. Randall had the suitcases taken to their new room.

"You go ahead. I'll be right there," Sage announced.

After the women walked away, Sage began methodically questioning the new desk clerk. She started out by asking him some simple questions like if he was a local, and how long he worked at the bed and breakfast. His name was Stephen, and he was born and raised in Moosehead.

He had only been at the job for two weeks. Working the night shift from three to eleven, he didn't get to talk to many of the other employees as the kitchen closed at nine and housekeeping was only on during the day. Meredith had hired him.

Sage asked him if he had ever seen the captain's ghost and he said he hadn't, but his brother had many years ago when they broke into the lighthouse before it became a new bed and breakfast. Pumping him for information, she kept talking because her new friend looked like he enjoyed having someone to talk to instead of being behind the desk at night by himself.

"Do you like working here?" Sage asked.

"I like the job, but between you and me I don't like Cassidy," he replied, looking around to make sure no one was near them. "She's a real know-it-all."

"What do you mean?"

"She screws up the reservations in the computer and then blames it on me. I try to show her how to do it, but she rolls her eyes and tells me she knows what she's doing when she doesn't."

"What do you mean she screws up the reservations? How?"

"She deletes guests' reservations and when they arrive, she refuses to give them a room. I've seen her do it. She deleted your reservation and the Simpson sisters, too. And when I called her out on it, she told me to mind my own business."

"Do the Randall's know she is doing it?"

"I don't think Mr. Randall does, but I know Meredith knows. I heard them talking one night about how double reservations make them money twice as fast and they just claim to be stupid about a computer glitch or they blame it on the previous owners. Please don't tell them I told you or I will lose my job. This is one of the higher paying jobs in the area and my family needs the money," Stephen begged.

"That's exactly what they said to us," Sage said. "Your secret is safe with me. Don't worry, I won't say a word."

"Do you like Mr. Randall?"

"He's nice but kind of dumb. I don't think he has a clue about what goes on around here. It seems to some of us that he didn't want to buy the bed and breakfast in the first place. Meredith doesn't take no for an answer, so I think he got roped into it."

"Are you saying Mr. Randall is not happy here or with his wife?"

"I know he's not happy here but it's not my place to say if he's happy with his wife or not. Although, the first time I saw him smile in a long time was when the sisters showed up. I think he knew one of them. She called him Donnie and they hugged for a real long time right here in the middle of the lobby."

"Was anyone around to see it happen?"

"Lots of people."

"Did Meredith see it?"

"She sure did, and man, she was spitting mad. After Mr. Randall left the area, she told the sisters they had no reservation and would have to leave. The older sister said they would call the police and file a complaint for stealing their money. It was then that Meredith gave them the room in the lighthouse."

"Why do you call Don, Mr. Randall, and Meredith by her first name?" Sage asked.

"I respect Mr. Randall even if he is a wuss when it comes to his wife. Meredith told me the first day she hired me I was to call her Meredith because being called Mrs. Randall made her skin crawl."

"Interesting," Sage mumbled. "It's been nice chatting with you. Will you be here tomorrow night?"

"Every night except for Tuesday and Wednesday. Those are my nights off."

"We'll be gone before then. We're only here for the long weekend. I'm afraid next year we will be going somewhere else for our vacation. It's not the same as it used to be now that Meredith has taken over."

"You're not the only ones saying that. I think this place is going to go out of business before it even has a chance to get off the ground," he said, frowning. "And I'll be out of a job again."

"Maybe Mr. Randall will step up and change things for the better. You never know," Sage said, "Have a good night."

CHAPTER THREE

The sun shone through the windows the next morning, warming the room. The women took turns using the one bathroom and were seated in the dining room by eight o'clock. Breakfast was set up buffet style.

A feast of different style eggs, waffles and various breakfast meats filled the main buffet table. On a second smaller table, home baked pastries, muffins, and pitchers of orange, apple, and cranberry juices were offered. A third table held hot beverages. Coffee, many different kinds of teas, and an espresso machine were available to the guests.

"Man, I would live here permanently if I could eat like this every day," Gabby said, filling her plate to the brim.

"Are you seriously going to eat all that?" Sage asked her friend.

"I'll burn the calories when we walk to town today," she answered, balancing a blueberry muffin on the side of her plate. "No judging me. I'm on vacation."

Everyone laughed as they set their plates on the table and went for beverages. Sage was the last one getting coffee. Meredith approached her while she was adding cream and sugar to her coffee.

"Can I help you with something, Meredith?" Sage asked as the woman moved into her personal space.

"I just want to tell you I'm watching you. I don't appreciate the fact that you took advantage of my husband's hospitality, and your group is now occupying two separate rooms. I wanted to charge you for another room and Donald wouldn't allow it," Meredith said in a low voice so the others in the dining room couldn't hear her.

"Remind me to thank your husband when I see him next," Sage said, stirring her coffee and hoping the woman would go away so she could enjoy her breakfast in peace.

"I also want you to stay away from my employees. Mind your own business and just enjoy your stay because it will be the last time you stay here."

"You can threaten me all you like," Sage said in an extremely loud voice. "And even if you said we could stay here for free next year we wouldn't ever return here again once this weekend is over."

The dining room chatter stopped, and all eyes were on Meredith and Sage. Word had circulated around the bed and breakfast about the body found in the lighthouse. Several guests had already checked out because of it and Meredith was not a happy person when she was losing money.

"You uppity…" Meredith started to say.

"Now excuse me while I rejoin my friends and enjoy my breakfast," Sage said, picking up her coffee mug and walking away.

"What was that all about?" Sarah asked her daughter while watching Meredith storm away.

"Just Meredith trying to strong arm her superiority over me," Sage replied. "It was nothing important. I just wanted to make my point that I wasn't afraid of her by speaking so loudly."

"She was pretty mad when she left," Gabby said.

"Let's not talk about Meredith anymore and just enjoy this wonderful food," Sage said, digging into her waffle covered in syrup, strawberries, and blueberries.

"While you two walk to town, we're going to

stretch out on the beach with a good book," Sarah said. "You have to promise to bring me back some fudge for Flora and Paul. I want to give her a small thank you gift for watching the shop while I'm gone."

"Some just for Flora?" her daughter asked sarcastically.

"Okay, some for me, too," Sarah said. "I like to freeze it and enjoy it over the winter months."

"While we're in town I want to stop at The Sea and Sand to check on Angie and make sure she's doing okay," Sage said. "You don't mind, do you Gabby?"

"Not in the least. Maybe we can check out the hotel while we are there, so we have a new place to go next year on our mini vacation," Gabby replied.

"Great idea. I love the area and would like to continue to come here if possible," Lou said.

"After breakfast I want to return my belongings to the bunk room in the lighthouse. Then we can go into town," Sage said to Gabby.

"Don't look now but the police are heading our way," Sarah said.

"Good morning, ladies. Do you mind if I join you?"

He pulled up a chair.

"I am Sheriff Carter. You dealt with my deputies

yesterday as I was out of the state on police business. Which one of you ladies was the one in the room when Beverly Simpson died?"

"I was in the room with her," Sarah replied.

Sage looked up and saw Meredith lurking at the door of the dining room. She was straining to hear what was being said. When she realized Sage was watching her, she hurried away.

"We are going to need you to come down to the station and file a formal report," he requested, leaning in closer to them. "The results came back on the earrings, and they were laced with cyanide."

"So Beverly was murdered?" Gabby whispered.

The sheriff motioned for them to stop talking when Cassidy grabbed a cup of coffee and sat down at the table next to them.

"Excuse me, would you please go sit at another table while I am here questioning possible witnesses?" Sheriff Carter said to the nosy desk clerk.

"I won't bother you," Cassidy replied.

"Maybe you don't think you will, but it will bother me to have someone nearby listening when I am trying to do my job," he said. 'Please move to another table."

Cassidy got up, left the coffee where it was and marched out of the room. Sage got up and followed her, stopping at the door to peek out. She reported directly to Meredith who was waiting for her twenty feet down the hallway.

"It didn't work, Meredith. You'll have to come up with a better plan next time," Sage said before turning and returning to the table.

"As I was saying to your mother, she is not a suspect. She was just in the wrong place at the wrong time. We have done background checks on all the employees and all the guests staying here. Everyone has been cleared except for the Randalls and their niece. We are still checking into their stories ever since Donald Randall came into the station and admitted he had an affair with the deceased person and his wife knew about it."

"Do you really think Meredith would be so stupid as to sign the note by name that came with the earrings?" Sage asked. "She's not the sharpest knife in the drawer, but still."

"I agree with you. It looks like someone is trying to frame her, but you never know. Maybe she did sign her name assuming we'd think the way we are about her being framed and it's all part of her plan," the sheriff replied. "Anyway, Sarah, please come to the station at your earliest convenience. The rest of you be careful and don't discuss the poisoned earrings with anyone."

"Your deputy already told us that and we won't," Lou said.

"Now, I'm going to go find Mrs. Randall and get some answers to some questions that I'm sure she won't want to answer," the sheriff said, standing up to leave. "I'm sorry about interrupting your breakfast. It looks delicious."

"It's nice to know you're in the clear," Lou said to Sarah. "I'm getting more coffee. Anyone need a refill?"

"I'll go with you. I need more coffee," Gabby said. grabbing her cup.

"I have to agree with Lou. It is nice that you're in clear, and we can enjoy the rest of our weekend," Sage said to her mother.

"Then what is bothering you? I can see it on your face."

"If it is one of the owners or their niece, what's to stop them from hurting or even killing someone else here?" Sage replied.

"There was a specific reason Beverly was murdered. I think Angie did the smart thing leaving here and staying somewhere else."

"I wonder if Angie knew of her sister's affair with Donald Randall?"

"More than likely, she did. Sisters share stuff like that between them."

"I'm going to ask her when we stop to check on her today," Sage replied. "If her sister went to school with Don then she must have at least known him."

"Don't go making this whole weekend about solving Beverly's murder. It has nothing to do with us and now that I am in the clear it really has nothing to do with us," Sarah said.

"I know, but I feel bad for Angie losing her sister the way she did and if Meredith did have something to do with it, I want her held responsible for it," Sage replied.

"I know it's useless to tell you not to get involved but at least try to enjoy some of the weekend."

"I will, I promise," Sage said, squeezing her mom's hand. "Now, I'm going back for more of that yummy bacon."

Half an hour later, Sage and Gabby were heading into town. Main Street was packed with people on vacation. The two friends visited several small gift shops before arriving at their main objective for their trip, The Fudge Factory.

They stopped just inside the door and deeply

inhaled the sweet smells that filled their nostrils. Children were running around, squealing with delight as they filled bags with candy while parents filled their own with their favorites. A large viewing window ran along the back wall allowing people to watch as the various candies were created.

An entire wall of wooden bins filled with many different flavors of saltwater taffy caught Gabby's eye first. She grabbed several lunch bag sized paper bags and started to fill them with a few pieces from each bin to get all the flavors offered.

Sage moved on to the penny candy wall. The prices weren't a penny anymore, but it was fun for Sage filling the bag as it brought her back to her childhood and their family vacations before her parents got divorced.

They joined forces when it came to the fudge wall. Sage got several of what the factory called a variety pound for her mother and one for Cliff. Chocolate, chocolate with nuts, penuche, and peanut butter fudge were included in the white boxes that were tied closed with red strings. She then got two boxes of penuche for herself; one for now and one to freeze for later. Gabby got the same for her mother, a pound of chocolate for Rory, and a variety box for herself.

They paid for their purchases, took their shopping bags, and forced themselves to leave the wonderful smells behind.

"Shall we do more shopping or check on Angie first?" Sage asked.

"Let's check on Angie. The hotel is right ahead of us. Then we have the rest of the day free to shop and eat," Gabby replied. "It's a good thing it's not too hot today or our fudge would melt."

"You're thinking of eating already? We just finished breakfast," Sage said, laughing.

"I know, but remember that little café we ate at last year? They had the best clam chowder and lobster rolls I have ever eaten. Just in case we don't come back next year, I want to eat there again."

They walked up to the front desk at The Sea and Sand and asked for Angie Simpson's room number. She was in room number 112.

"I thought this was a hotel not a motel," Sage said as they walked to the rear of the building where Angie's room was located.

They knocked on the door and heard a commotion inside.

"I'll be right there," they heard Angie say from inside the room. "Hold on a second."

"Who's there?" Angie asked, opening the door a few inches and peering out.

"It's just us. We were stopping by to check on you and make sure you were okay," Sage replied.

They heard someone moving around in the room behind Angie and then a door closed.

"I'm fine. I'm waiting for the coroner to release my sister's body and then I'll be taking her home," Angie said, nervously, keeping a firm hold on the door.

"Did they give you any time frame of when that would be?" Gabby asked.

"He said within the next few days, probably Tuesday. Other than that, I haven't heard a thing from him or the police," Angie replied.

"Can we come in?" Sage asked.

"No, I'd rather be by myself right now. I appreciate you checking on me, I really do, but please respect my privacy and let me grieve in peace."

"Okay. We're heading back to the bed and breakfast right now so if you need us you can reach us there. Again, we're very sorry about your sister," Sage said.

"Thank you," Angie said, closing the door in their faces.

"Well, that was rude," Gabby said. "Why did you

tell her we were going back to the bed and breakfast?"

"Because someone was in the room with her, she didn't want us to see. Didn't you hear them moving around and closing a door behind her?"

"I did. Maybe it's a family member," Gabby suggested.

"I don't know. But if she thinks we went back to the B&B and she lets her guard down, we can hang around and they may come out of the room so we can see who she was hiding," Sage replied. "There's a cabana bar on the beach at the rear of the motel. We can sit there and have some iced tea while we watch the door of the room."

"I could have something to drink. I'm in," Gabby replied.

They ordered and sat where they had a clear view of room 112. It wasn't long before the door opened. Angie stepped out, looked around and signaled for whoever was in the room to come out. To their surprise, Cassidy, the front desk clerk, exited and hurried down the street.

"What is she doing here?" Gabby asked.

"I don't know but when we return to the bed and breakfast I will find out," Sage said. "Are you ready to go shopping?"

"I am. I saw a shop on Main Street that had arrowhead necklaces in the front window. Rory has collected them since he was a young boy and I thought I might pick up a necklace for him," Gabby replied.

"Cliff is so hard to buy for. He doesn't collect much of anything and doesn't have any hobbies. He works so hard on his parent's farm that he doesn't have time for much else," Sage said. "Don't get me wrong, he loves what he does but farm life is very time consuming."

"He is a hard worker. There's got to be something we can find for him. Maybe they'll have something in the same shop as the arrowhead necklaces," Gabby suggested.

The shop mainly specialized in gifts for men. Gabby found a beautiful sterling silver arrowhead necklace with a turquoise inlay for her fiancé and had it giftwrapped. They continued to walk up and down, peering into the display cases looking for something for Cliff.

In the very last case, Sage found what she was looking for. A sterling silver farm tractor on a box chain was the perfect gift for her new boyfriend.

"He'll love it," Gabby said, walking up behind her friend.

The clerk took the tractor out of the case and Sage followed her to the register. While she stood at the counter waiting for the gift to be wrapped, Sage glanced out the window and spotted Angie walking on the opposite side of the street and she wasn't alone.

"Isn't that Don Randall?" Gabby asked.

"It sure is. Why would he be with Angie?" Sage asked.

"Maybe he's checking on her like we did."

"Could be. They don't seem to be hiding the fact they are together," Sage replied.

"First Cassidy and now Don. Angie seems to have become quite popular, hasn't she?"

"Yea, for someone who was discarded to the bunk room in the lighthouse, now she seems very much in demand," Sage said, watching them until they were out of sight.

"Are you hungry yet? I'm famished," Gabby said. "Let's go get those lobster rolls and enjoy some of our vacation without thinking about a murder."

"I'm sorry. Those lobster rolls are calling our names," Sage said, thanking the clerk and picking up the bag. "Lead the way to the café."

The two friends ate outside in the sunshine on the café patio. The clam chowder was creamy and so thick you could tilt the spoon and it stayed put. The lobster rolls were set on the table. The toasted hotdog rolls had a bed of lettuce at the bottom and were spilling over with lobster meat mixed in a light coating of mayonnaise.

"I will never finish all this," Sage said. "The bowl of chowder all but did me in."

"It's only a short walk back and you have the fridge in your room so it will keep until you decide to snack on it later," Gabby said, digging into her food. "I have died and gone to heaven."

"You can eat more than me and Cliff combined yet you never gain any weight," Sage commented.

"It's all in the genes. Look at my mom. She doesn't have an ounce of fat on her, and she eats more than I do," Gabby said through a mouthful of lobster.

"I bet Meredith sent Cassidy to see Angie," Sage said, thinking out loud as she picked at her lunch. "But why?"

"You just can't get a mystery out of your mind, can you?"

"As you say, it's in the genes. My mom loves mysteries and the paranormal and she passed it on to me."

"I guess we're all peas in a pod," Gabby replied.

After lunch the two friends headed back to take an

afternoon dip in the ocean. As they walked along the street Sage happened to glance in a shop window and spotted an item that caught her eye.

"Come on," she said, grabbing her friend's arm and pulling her into the shop with her.

Sage approached the clerk and asked about the lighthouse earrings displayed in the window. They were the exact ones that had been sent to Beverly.

"Does anyone else carry those specific earrings in the town?" Sage asked.

"No, they are exclusive to our shop only."

"Do you sell a lot of them?" Sage asked.

"Yes, we do. They are one of our best sellers."

"You don't deliver, do you?"

"No, we don't. I'm so sorry," the clerk replied.

"That's okay, thank you for your help," Sage said.

"It's funny. You are the second ones who came in here asking about delivery of those specific earrings."

"Who else inquired about them?" Sage asked, hoping it was the person who bought them and wanted the shop to deliver them to their bed and breakfast.

"The police were in here asking the same questions you are," the clerk replied.

"Okay, Thanks again," Sage said.

"We know where the earrings came from," Gabby said once they were outside.

"And we know it wasn't anyone at the shop who delivered them, so whoever bought them put them outside the door themselves or had someone do it for them."

"Maybe that person didn't know what they were delivering," Gabby suggested.

"Could be, but I have a feeling whoever bought them delivered them."

"Anyone could have bought them," Gabby said. "They are on display in a window on Main Street."

"True, but whoever did had a reason to, and that reason was murder. Premeditated murder. Hold on a second. I'll be right back," Sage said, running back into the shop.

She returned a moment later, frowning.

"What's up? Why did you go back in there?"

"I thought maybe if they had a camera we could see if we knew anyone who had been shopping in there or purchased the earrings. But they don't have a working camera, only a fake one to deter people from shoplifting," Sage replied. "It was above the door pointing into the shop. I didn't notice it when we left."

"If they had a camera the police would have confiscated the video already," Gabby said.

"I didn't think of that," Sage admitted. "Let's go swimming."

After changing in their respective rooms, the friends met up and walked down to the beach. Lou and Sarah were perched in beach chairs on the water's edge with their feet dangling in the cool water. Both were reading and had a glass of wine in the cup holder of their chair. Sage and Gabby set their beach bags and towels next to their moms and ran into the ocean for an afternoon dip. After a half an hour swim, they spread out their blankets on the sand and sunbathed.

"Can you believe they charged us a dollar an hour to rent the chairs?" Lou said. "These people are not going to be in business very long the way they nickel and dime their guests."

"Don said his wife was going to do everything possible to make this place profitable, even if he doesn't agree with all her policies," Sage replied. "This place would be a lot better run with Don in charge but Stephen at the desk said he didn't want to buy it in the first place."

"It's makes you wonder why he gave in to her, doesn't it?" Lou asked, setting her book down in her lap to converse.

"Did you get my fudge?" Sarah asked.

"I did. It is safely tucked away in the room where it's cool," Sage answered. "And wait until you see what I picked up for Cliff."

"We also discovered that Angie Simpson has quite the social life with her sister gone," Gabby said.

"Do tell," Lou said.

"We stopped at the hotel like we said we were going to and checked on Angie. She wouldn't let us in, and we could hear someone moving around in the room behind her. So, we waited and watched, and guess who came out of the room?" Sage asked.

"Who?"

"Cassidy, Meredith's niece. We watched the room until someone came out."

"Why would she be visiting Angie?" Lou asked.

"We don't know yet, but it was really obvious that Angie didn't want anyone to know she was there. And then as we were shopping down Main Street, we saw her and Don Randall walking together on the opposite side of the street."

"Well, isn't that interesting," Lou stated.

"I pointed out to Sage that maybe he had gone to check on her like we did," Gabby said.

"Or maybe he's afraid of being sued," Sarah added.

"That could be. By sticking the sisters out in the bunk room of the lighthouse there was no way anyone could watch the room and he did say he felt responsible for Beverly's death," Sage replied.

"He felt responsible because of the affair," Lou reminded her.

"It seems like everything always goes back to Meredith. She was the one who put the sisters out in the lighthouse in the first place like she did to us."

"But Stephen said it was Cassidy who was cancelling people's reservations. Maybe she did it on purpose so the sisters would be placed out there," Lou said.

"But did she do it under Meredith's direction?" Sage asked. "The whole thing makes no sense. Angie said they didn't know about the new owners until they got here. Could Meredith have seen their name on the list of reservations from last year and planned this whole thing in advance?"

"You're right. It does seem to all lead back to Meredith," Gabby said. "But the big question is why would she sign her own name to the note?"

"I don't know. But for the next hour or so I'm going to enjoy the beach and not think about the murder of Beverly Simpson," Sarah stated, closing her eyes and laying her head on the back of the beach chair.

The rest of the afternoon was spent dipping in and out of the ocean and sun tanning. An hour before their assigned dining time they headed in from the beach for showers. They met in the lobby and took a table at the front of the dining room.

The night's menu offered seafood, and Italian food. Sage and Gabby ordered veal parmigiana with linguine, Sarah ordered shrimp scampi, and Lou had another go at a fisherman's platter. After eating, they went into the bar for a nightcap before retiring to their rooms. The fresh air and sun had got the better of them and each woman had a sunburn despite using sun block. They decided to go to bed early and spend the entire day on the beach the following day.

Sarah settled in immediately and was asleep in minutes. Sage couldn't get comfortable because of her sunburn so she decided to take a walk in the cool night air. The outdoor patio was full of guests who had taken their drinks outside to socialize. It was too noisy for Sage, so she turned around and walked in the other direction to the front of the lighthouse.

"Want some company?" her mother asked, coming up behind her.

"I didn't wake you up, did I?"

"No, I woke up to use the bathroom and saw you weren't in the room. I figured maybe we could do a little ghost hunting together. If you're game that is."

"The captain's ghost is mainly seen in the lighthouse. Shall we start in there?"

"I have my recorder and my EMF meter ready to go," Sarah said. "I hope this is the year I see him as I don't think we will be returning here ever again."

"Maybe he heard you and will show himself," Sage said.

They entered through the base door but instead of going straight ahead to the bunk room they took a hard right and headed for the metal stairs that led to the top of the lighthouse. They stopped at each window along the way looking out over the surrounding town. The display of lights from the various businesses all the way to downtown Moosehead was spectacular.

Halfway up to the top they stopped to look out another window.

"Do you hear that?" Sage asked her mom.

CHAPTER FOUR

The two women were standing still but footsteps could be heard coming up the metal stairs behind them. They stopped talking and flattened themselves against the wall of the lighthouse. The sound of the footsteps was coming closer and closer to the mother and daughter.

A breeze of cold air passed by them giving them goosebumps. The sounds of the footsteps echoed up the stairs past them.

"Captain Wells, is that you that just passed by us?" Sarah asked, turning on her recorder.

Silence.

"You do know your story was told and they know who it was who murdered you. You don't have to stay here anymore. You are free to go into the light and move on," Sarah said.

Silence.

Twenty feet ahead of them, a light began to form on the stairs. At first it was a small ball of soft white light, an orb, and it grew into the shape and size of a full-grown man.

"Mom," Sage stammered.

"I see him," she calmly replied.

A man dressed in a long waistcoat with gold buttons and a black seaman's hat materialized before them. He had a full beard and piercing dark eyes. A fancy brass telescope was tucked under one arm. He was identical to the portrait that was in the lobby above the check-in desk. It was the ghost of Captain Wells.

His mouth was moving as if he was speaking but the women could hear no words. He tipped his hat to them, smiled, and turned to continue climbing the stairs. Each footstep became more distant until finally they ceased all together. His light diminished back into a small orb, and it shot up the stairs out of sight. The two women stood there, frozen on the steps, trying to process what they had just witnessed.

"Thank you, Captain Wells. I hope you find some

peace," Sarah finally said. "Let's get back to the room. I want to play back the recorder."

"I can't believe he showed himself to us," Sage replied. "That's the first ghost I have ever seen."

"We were no threat to him. I don't think he had been told the story of his death was known. Didn't the pamphlet say he was here because he needed people to know that he was murdered? Maybe now he can move on because I don't think Meredith will treat him or the lighthouse with any respect."

Back in the room they played the recording. Words could be heard here and there but they were very hard to make out as to what the ghost was saying. The one thing that did stand out loud and clear was a thank you ma'am that followed right after Sarah said his story had been told and he could move on.

"This was an amazing night," Sage said, crawling into bed. "I am so glad you got to see Captain Wells on your last stay here."

"We had never gone up into the lighthouse before tonight. I hope he can move on now, but sometimes they just decide to stay where they feel they belong and are still needed. But you're right, it was an amazing night and I'm glad I got to share it with my daughter," Sarah said, yawning. "Wait until I tell Lou in the morning what happened to us. She won't believe it. Good thing I have the recording of his voice."

"It's a good thing Gabby is staying in the main part of the bed and breakfast. She would never get any sleep knowing a ghost was walking around in the lighthouse right outside the bunk room door," Sage said, laughing. "Good night, Mom. Love you."

"Love you more," Sarah said, closing her eyes.

The next morning was Sunday and their last day there. The four friends met for breakfast. Sarah had her recorder in hand and gushed at the news they had finally seen the captain's ghost after all these years. She played the voice recordings for them while they ate. The first words out of Gabby's mouth were she was glad she wasn't sleeping out there anymore. Sarah laughed as she told her Sage knew that was exactly what she would say when she found out the ghost really existed.

"We have to be out of our rooms by five o'clock," Lou said. "What shall we do on our last day here?"

"I vote we spend it on the beach. It's supposed to be gorgeous today and I would like to finish my book before we leave," Sarah replied.

"I can finish working on my tan," Gabby said.

"Lord knows I won't be able to lounge around in the sunshine after I return to work at the salon."

"You guys can enjoy the beach. I don't want to leave here without knowing who and why Beverly was killed. I'm going to question Cassidy and find out why she was at Angie's motel and then I am going back to see Angie and ask her why she was with Don Randall," Sage said.

"You shouldn't go by yourself," Lou aid.

"I'll be fine. And I can join you later at the farewell buffet in the bar," Sage replied. "I heard the spread is incredible."

"I heard the same thing. It amazes me that Meredith would spend money to create a buffet like that but maybe she's hoping it will be the last thing people remember and return to stay again," Gabby replied.

"Are you sure you can't spend the day on the beach with us?" Sage's mom asked.

"You know when Sage gets a mystery on her mind she can't let it go," Gabby said.

"She could let the police figure it out and read about it in the Moosehead Beacon," Sarah said. "But I know better. My daughter won't be happy until she figures out who did it."

"I'm taking a cup of coffee to go and getting into my bathing suit," Lou said, standing up.

"I'm right behind you, Mom," Gabby replied.

"Please be extra careful," Sarah said to Sage, giving her a hug.

"I'll be out in public the whole time with lots of people around. I'll see you at brunch."

Sage approached the front desk where Cassidy was busy with another couple checking out early. She was pleasant to the patrons, a complete change from the Cassidy Sage had witnessed when they were checking in. They picked up their suitcases and walked away leaving Sage next in line. Cassidy looked up and frowned when she saw Sage.

"Are you checking out early?" she asked.

"No, I have a few questions to ask you."

"Meredith told me I didn't have to answer any of your questions or even talk to you," Cassidy replied.

"No, you don't, but wouldn't you like to see your aunt's business succeed?"

"That's a dumb question, of course I would," Cassidy snapped.

"Well, if there are any more dead people found on the premises no one will stay here out of fear, and the business will fail, and you will be out a job."

"I never thought of that. I like this job," she said.

"My aunt said I have to work on my people skills and if I do that I can stay here working for her."

And then Sage saw them. The same lighthouse earrings were dangling from Cassidy's ears that had been gifted to Beverly before she died.

"I love your earrings. Where did you get them?" Sage asked.

"They were a gift from a friend, and I don't know where she got them," Cassidy replied, suspicious of Sage's change of demeanor.

"I've never seen them on you before," Sage said, pushing on in her questioning.

"That's because I just received them yesterday," Cassidy said, fingering the earrings.

Sage decided to lay it all out on the line.

"Did Angie give them to you when you were at her motel yesterday?"

"How do you know I was there?"

"Gabby and I stopped to check on Angie to make sure she was doing okay, and we heard someone in the room with her when she opened the door. We were sitting at a cabana having a drink, cooling off and we saw you leave the room Why did you hide from us?"

"I didn't want to. Angie told me to be quiet while she answered the door, so I did what she said to do."

"What were you doing there?"

"Mrs. Randall asked me to bring her suitcase to her at the motel. The police said they were done with it, and she wanted it out of the bed and breakfast. I delivered it to her, and she gave me the earrings as a thank you."

"So Angie gave you the earrings?"

"I just said that didn't I?" Cassidy said, rolling her eyes.

Don Randall walked up to the desk as the two women were chatting. He greeted Sage and turned to say something to Cassidy. The smile on his face disappeared, and he stared at the desk clerk. His posture became rigid, and he excused himself, hurrying away. Sage knew she had to follow him and see why he became so upset.

Don entered his office and immediately made a phone call. The door was left open a couple of inches and Sage edged as close to the door as she dared to so she could listen. His back was to her, and she couldn't make out what he was saying. He hung up and she hurried up the hallway so as not to get caught eaves-dropping.

Sage sat in the lobby for a few minutes to see if Don Randall would come out of his office and go anywhere but he never left. Her next step was to talk to Angie. She left for town on foot and arrived at the motel twenty minutes later.

She stopped at the front desk to see if Angie was still registered, and she was.

"I'm her cousin and heard Beverly died up the street at the Moosehead Lighthouse Bed and Breakfast," Sage said to the clerk. "I'm splitting the cost of the room with Angie while I am here and I know she came here the same day her sister died. What day did she check in?"

"It looks like she checked in this past Friday, but she had the room reserved for a week prior to her arrival. It's our busiest time of year and she wanted to make sure she had a room."

"I'm not paying for a whole week when I wasn't even here," Sage replied.

"She already paid for the room in advance. You'll have to straighten things out with your cousin."

"That's odd," Sage mumbled. "It's like she knew she would need the room."

"Excuse me?" the clerk asked.

"Oh, nothing. Thank you for your help. She's still in room 112, correct?" Sage said, turning to walk away.

"She is," the clerk replied.

Sage hurried to the rear of the motel. As she

turned the last corner, she spotted someone she knew so she ducked behind a large potted plant to watch. Meredith Randall headed straight for room 112 and knocked on the door. She looked around nervously as if she didn't want to be seen. Angie finally answered the door and Meredith pushed in through the open door.

I'm going to find out what is going on in that room.

Sage stood close to the door and could hear the two women arguing inside. Meredith was doing most of the screaming. They seemed to be arguing about Donald Randall. She pressed her ear flat against the door hoping to hear what they were saying more clearly. After listening for a while longer she figured the whole mess out.

A noise behind her made her turn around. Donald Randall stood there. That was the last thing she remembered before she hit the ground.

CHAPTER FIVE

Sage woke up in a groggy state. She was lying on a bed, hands tied behind her back. Next to her, Meredith lay unconscious and bound. In the back of the room, Donald, Cassidy, and Angie were deep in conversation. Sage closed her eyes so they wouldn't know she was conscious and listening.

"Now we have two bodies to get rid of," Donald said. "What were you thinking calling Meredith and telling her to come here? What happened to framing her and letting her rot in jail?"

"Things weren't moving fast enough for my liking," Angie said.

"I planted the cyanide bottle in her jewelry box like we talked about. The autopsy was only a short time from being completed and the cops would have come nosing around the bed and breakfast and found the bottle. You might have screwed this whole thing up by rushing things," Donald said.

"Look, it's bad enough I killed my own sister to be with you," Angie replied.

"So now you think it's my turn to kill Meredith to be with you?" Donald asked. "Sorry to disappoint you but I'm no killer."

"This works out for the better. I'll give Meredith a dose of cyanide and write a suicide note stating she couldn't take the guilt after killing Beverly out of jealousy. Tonight, after it gets dark you can bring your wife back to the bed and breakfast and put her on the bathroom floor with the suicide note next to her, and then go to bed. You can conveniently find her in the morning and call the police."

"And we each have taken out a life insurance policy on the other one, but Meredith's policy won't be paid because it is a suicide," Donald stated.

"Not to worry. My sister's policy is for two million dollars. I took it out years ago so nothing will seem fishy. I think we can move to Europe and live quite comfortably on the one payout," Angie said. "If she only knew before she died that we were just using her to cover up our own affair. Meredith was always watching you to make sure you stayed away from

Beverly, and it made it so easy for us to sneak away and spend time together. Now we don't have to sneak around anymore."

"And I get to run the bed and breakfast like it is my own," Cassidy added to the conversation.

I wondered how she was involved in this.

"After we are out of the country with the insurance money I will sign the business over to you," Donald said. "It's the least I can do for you for delivering the earrings in the first place."

"I always wanted my own business," Cassidy said.

"This is all great but what about the other one?" Donald asked. "What are we going to do with her body?"

"Doesn't the bed and breakfast have a boat you rent out? There are a lot of sharks in the water this time of year. A few sleeping pills and we'll tie her to a couple of cement blocks and drop her out in the ocean tonight," Angie replied.

"But her party is due to check out by five. They'll notice when she doesn't return for the farewell brunch," Donald argued.

"She came to town by herself. Who's to say what happened to her while she was here," Angie replied. "You two return to the hotel and go about your business and let me prepare everything on this end."

Several loud knocks shook the door.

"POLICE! OPEN UP!"

The three stood frozen at the back of the room. Cassidy was the first to move, running for the bathroom and locking the door.

"OPEN UP OR WE'LL BUST IT IN!"

"Now what do we do?" Donald asked in a panic.

"Help!" Sage yelled. "Help us!"

The police broke through the door as Angie was fighting to get the bathroom door open.

"Down on the floor, both of you!"

Another officer cuts the binds around Sage's hands.

"Call in the paramedics," another officer said into his shoulder radio, while checking on Meredith.

Sage sat up on the bed and watched as the two were cuffed.

"Cassidy Black is in on it too, and she's in the bathroom," Sage said.

"We got her as she climbed out the window," the officer assured her.

"You have nothing on us," Angie screamed as they stood her up.

"That's where you are wrong," Sage said, taking her mother's small tape recorder out of her back pocket. "It was nice of you to tie my hands behind my back so I could turn it on and record every word you said."

"All this planning for nothing," Angie hissed at Sage as she was led out in handcuffs.

"Is Meredith okay?" Sage asked the paramedics.

"She's got a nasty bump on the head, but I think she'll be okay. We're going to take her to the hospital just to be sure. Do you need to go and be checked out?"

"I'm good, just a bit of a headache."

Sage sat on the bed while they took Meredith out on a gurney. The officer in charge asked for the tape recorder and Sage turned it over to him.

"How did you know I was here?" she asked.

"Hold on," he said, walking to the door and waving to someone.

Gabby walked through the door. Sage ran to her friend and hugged her fiercely.

"You followed me?"

"I did. Right after you left I saw Donald leave, too. Something told me to follow him, and I saw him talking to you at the motel door. Cassidy came up behind you and whacked you in the head and they both dragged you into the room. I called the sheriff and waited for them to arrive," Gabby said.

"I could kiss you! If it wasn't for you I would be shark food," Sage said, hugging her friend again.

"Just do me a favor. Don't go looking for trouble on your own again because next time I might not be so brave," Gabby replied.

"I'll need you both to come to the station and file a formal report before you leave the area," the officer told them.

"We'll be there later this afternoon. Let's go back to the bed and breakfast," Sage said, wrapping her arm around her friend.

"Do you want a ride?"

"I've never ridden in a police car before. Can we?" Gabby asked, turning to Sage.

They climbed into the police car and rode back to the bed and breakfast with lights blazing. The other guests flocked to the front of the building when the vehicle pulled into the circular driveway. The friends exited the car looking for their moms, but they weren't among the crowd of onlookers.

"I bet they are out on the beach," Gabby said.

"Before you leave, do you know who is in charge under the Randalls?" the officer asked.

"We don't," Sage answered for both of them.

"That's okay, I'll find out. Don't forget to come to the station later," he said. walking off.

The crowd gathered around them trying to find out why they were riding in a police car, but the women just wanted to go find their moms and tell them what happened. They pushed through the throng and headed out to the beach.

They found Sarah and Lou sitting on the beach, sipping wine, happily chatting amongst themselves totally unaware of what had happened in town. Sitting down in the sand in front of them, they told their moms the whole story.

Sarah was upset that her daughter was hurt and couldn't believe that Donald Randall was in on the whole thing as he seemed so nice. Lou was even more upset because Gabby followed the owner without telling anyone and could also have been hurt in the process.

"I guess Meredith will be the sole owner of the bed and breakfast now. I wonder how long it will stay open," Gabby said.

"I don't know, but what I do know is we have a buffet to go to before we leave. I for one am starving and after all that has happened here this weekend I need a good final memory of this place."

The women parted ways. They all showered and

changed for the buffet. Their suitcases were packed and put in their car before they went to the bar to eat.

"This buffet is awesome, just as advertised. I'm going to bust if I eat everything I want to try," Gabby said, filling her plate.

With full plates and full wine glasses, they settled into a far corner for a little bit of privacy while they ate.

"It's too bad we won't be returning here next year. Over the years I've come to like this place," Lou said, popping a calamari ring into her mouth.

"I hope you will return next year," Meredith said, coming up behind them. "And every year after that, free of charge."

"Excuse me?" Sarah asked.

"The police told me everything and I didn't believe my husband was involved until I heard the recording Sage made. Your daughters saved my life, and I will be forever grateful. I'm sorry I was so nasty when you first arrived. I had just dealt with the sisters showing up and was in a very foul mood. I'm normally not so rude. Please accept my apologies and tell me you will return next year," Meredith replied.

"We will," Sarah said. "And thank you."

Meredith walked away perusing the buffet to make sure all was well, and everything was full.

Sarah looked at her daughter and Sage knew she would have to confess to what she did.

"You made a recording?"

"I'm so sorry, Mom. I brought your recorder with me in case something happened. I'm afraid I taped over the evidence of Captain Wells speaking to us. I know you were going to bring it to your paranormal group meeting, and I destroyed it," Sage said, frowning. "Can you forgive me after waiting all those years to finally see the captain?"

"Forgive you? If that recording puts those three away for a very long time it will be worth the loss. Besides, now that Meredith has invited us back again, you and I can stay out in the bunk house. Maybe we'll see him again and next time I'll catch his image on my phone."

"So you're not mad?" Sage asked.

"Nah. You and I saw him and that's what is important. If no one else believes me, that's their problem," Sarah said. "I have my daughter to continue my ghost hunting with and that's what's important to me. It's all about the chase."

"That's a weight off my mind. Now, let's eat!" Sage said.

Printed in Great Britain
by Amazon

Recovering from Divorce or Separation

These notes are based on *Breaking Up Without Cracking Up* by Christopher Compston (HarperCollins 1998, £6.99)

It would be useful to read the book in advance. These talks are interdependent so please try to attend them all.

You may find the first week particularly difficult but, even if you are already divorced, or separated, it is essential to consider your past relationships, painful though this may be. Don't despair – there is light at the end of the tunnel – the gospel is a gospel of hope.

First published 2000

Published by HTB Publications, Holy Trinity Brompton, Brompton Road, London SW7 1JA

Contents

Week 1

Getting Our Priorities Right

Introduction

- Talks designed to help injured parties (including children, family, friends) and the helpers – often we are both.

- Based on biblical principles, with generous doses of common sense.

1. Get priorities right

The ideal order is:

- God

- Partner

- Children

- Work

- Hobbies or other interests

2. Importance of other relationships

Especially with parents, brothers and sisters

3. Importance of commitment

'Murder often – divorce never!'

4. What hinders relationships?

- Lack of time
- Failure to communicate – not listening
- Other people

What helps?

- Prayer
- Rest and fun
- Feelings more than thoughts
- A stitch in time

Note

Serious specific problems such as abuse, violence, addictive behaviour, alcoholism and sexual perversions require professional help – and real quick!

Notes

_____

_____

_____

_____

_____

_____

_____

_____

_____

_____

_____

_____

_____

_____

_____

_____

_____

_____

_____

_____

_____

_____

Notes

_____

_____

_____

_____

_____

_____

_____

_____

_____

_____

_____

_____

_____

_____

_____

_____

_____

_____

_____

5. Is it such a good idea?

Should I divorce? Should I separate?

Personal points to ponder

- Have I really done all I can? Have I really thought, discussed, waited, tried?

- Have I really considered the children more than myself?

Worth making every effort to reconcile

Divorce and separation should be the last resort

Why?

It brings:

- Pain

- Grief

- Guilt

- Anger

- Loneliness

- Financial problems

- Damage to children

Death is final: divorce and separation are not

It is a process

Week 2

During Divorce or Separation

Still try to reconcile. Last minute reconciliation can happen

If inevitable, be a surgeon, not a butcher

Professional help

1. Solicitors

Choose with great care

2. Counsellors

Don't swop around. Must respect them. Choose couples or same sex

3. Friends

Small loyal circle. Don't tell the world. Beware of false friends

Notes

_____

_____

_____

_____

_____

_____

_____

_____

_____

_____

_____

_____

_____

_____

_____

_____

'As far as the east is from the west, so far has he removed our transgressions from us' **(Psalm 103:12).**

_____

First aid when the crunch comes

Feet on the ground

How can I help myself?

1. Love yourself. Learn to live with yourself

2. Dealing with guilt

3. Dealing with anger

4. Appreciate you are in a grief situation. It will not last forever. Healing takes time. Convalescence. Take each day as it comes

5. Appreciate others have problems. Avoid self pity

6. Gentle involvement outside, including other grandparents. Minor hobbies, easy commitments

7. Laughter

8. No deep emotional relationships – not yet!

9. Prayer – prayer – prayer

Forgiveness

Essential. Why?

We ourselves have been forgiven much

By holding on to our grievances

bitterly, we get stuck and cannot begin healing and moving on with life

Note

Forgiveness is an act of will, not an emotion

Notes

_____

_____

_____

_____

_____

_____

_____

_____

_____

_____

_____

_____

_____

_____

_____

_____

_____

_____

_____

_____

_____

_____

_____

_____

_____

_____

_____

_____

_____

_____

_____

_____

_____

_____

_____

_____

Week 3

Following Divorce or Separation

Love

Some hints for the helper

Remember, having lost the person nearest to them, those injured need your love more than ever, possibly for a long time.

1. Listen – listen – listen

2. Confidentiality

3. 'Accept' – even if it seems difficult

But is there an underlying personal problem?

4. Be inclusive – divorce and separation disrupt most social relationships

Gentle challenges – get them out of self-centred gloom

5. Encourage

6. Don't be judgmental – see both sides but don't condone

7. Money

8. Hospitality

9. Time
What about your children?

The priority

A damage limitation exercise

Underlying aim, a good relationship
with both parents. This aids their
recovery and yours.

1. Ideally, both parents tell them
straight, according to their age, but not
the grisly details

2. Stress divorce and separation is not
their fault

3. Love them, don't spoil. Emotional
blackmail. Be a parent, not a pal

4. Generous access – live nearby if
possible. Keep in contact, however
painful

5. Never criticise other parent

6. Don't pump for information

More hints for the helper

If you can't face the parents at least
help the children. Your own children

Notes

_____

_____

_____

_____

_____

_____

_____

_____

_____

_____

_____

_____

_____

_____

_____

_____

_____

_____

_____

Notes

_____

_____

_____

_____

_____

_____

_____

_____

_____

_____

_____

_____

_____

_____

_____

_____

_____

can help too:

How about the following?

1. Standing in for parents or grandparents

2. Talking of and to the absent parent

3. Making your home available for access visits.

Week 4

Looking Forward to the Future

- In a sense there is no after. At least, not yet. It is a continuing process. Your attitude is crucial

- Decree Absolute or the final separation – anti-climax. Still work to be done

Tying up loose ends

Both partners

1. Emotional spring cleaning

Letting go of the past. Your ex is not your property nor your problem

2. Practical spring cleaning

3. Tidying up loose ends; no unfinished business eg holiday cottage, dividing furniture

The Children

Remember they are the priority

Establish flexible pattern, agree as much

Notes

_____

_____

_____

_____

_____

_____

_____

_____

_____

_____

_____

_____

_____

_____

_____

_____

_____

_____

_____

_____

_____

Notes

_____

_____

_____

_____

_____

_____

_____

_____

_____

_____

_____

_____

_____

_____

_____

_____

_____

_____

_____

as possible. The older the children, more their choice. Keep up access, whatever pain or problem. Their needs are very important.

1. Don't outlaw the in-laws – rebuild links also with friends if possible

2. Challenge yourself. Get involved generously – look outward, not inward

3. Forgiveness

Start practising forgiveness. It's a decision not a feeling

Bitterness is a cancer. For your own sake don't let the past taint the future

4. Then – and only then – new deep relationship

And the helpers?

1. All the former points apply. Your help may be more important than before

2. Parties less outspoken but still desperate. Possibly more so now that drama is over

3. Older, poorer with damaged children, probably in smaller house. Different place. Different school. Woman may not have worked or had independent life for many years. Much

easier for a man than a woman

4. So keep your loving support up gently edging your friends towards health and happiness, reminding them that other kinds of human relationship can be very rewarding

New relationships

Hasten slowly, let the wounds heal, the grief be worked through. Above all, try to learn to live with yourself as an independent individual under God. Only then can you properly contemplate living with someone else.

1. The single life

Many advantages

2. A new relationship?

- Your new partner is likely to be older, possibly more bruised by life than your first

- If unmarried, not used to the hurly burly of family life with children so take it slowly

- If widowed, sufficiently recovered? You must allow space for memories of the past

Notes

Notes

_____

_____

_____

_____

_____

_____

_____

_____

_____

_____

_____

_____

_____

_____

_____

_____

_____

*'The Lord bless you and keep you: the Lord
make his face to shine upon you, and be
gracious to you: the Lord lift up his
countenance upon you, and give you peace'*
(Numbers 6:24-26).

_____

- If divorced, sufficiently recovered? If not, be cautious!

3. Children

Remember that children face more upheaval through their parents' new relationship than they did when their parents lived alone with them

Step-children

What a subject! Essentially, remember that you are not and never can be their parent so don't try too hard

Different standards: different homes

You must respect their relationship with their own parents and must allow them space and time with their parent even if now with you

For encouragement, read the book of Ruth

Post Script

Suffering – why me?

No easy answer but suffering can make you or break you